Caleb J. Ross—
Murmurs
gathered stories vol. one

Viscera

Irrational

Originally published by Viscera Irrational

Cover design and internal layout, Caleb J. Ross
Cover image used under Creative Commons license (creativecommons.org/licenses/by/2.0). Credit: flickr.com/photos/linhngan/

ISBN-13: 978-0615954066

Produced in the United States of America

The stories collected in Murmurs: Gathered Stories Vol. One first appeared in altered form—sometimes slightly, sometimes drastically—in the following publications. The author thanks each and every eyeball responsible for giving these stories their first audiences.

Click-Clack first appeared in Warmed and Bound, Petty Injuries first appeared at Dogmatika, Legs Unwilling first appeared at Rotten Leaves, Formaldehyde (excerpted from Stranger Will) first appeared at Red Fez, Born Again Michael first appeared in Eternal Night: a Vampire Anthology, It Sparks first appeared in Sideshow Fables, Car Dodging first appeared at No Record Press, Snake Girl at Scab first appeared at 3:AM Magazine, Norman Rockwell Nostalgia first appeared in partial form at Full of Crow

Section One: Superior Vena Cava

Section Two: Aorta

Section One: Superior Vena Cava

Click-Clack

Some say the train's click-clack echoed his mother's escape, that the looming engine overtook and ultimately replaced the sound of her footsteps, leaving Ernie with only the train's passing heat for warmth and its lumbering weight to serve as the heartbeat he had nestled for the past nine months.

When Jack found the baby, newborn and discarded, webbed among the weeds and other failed carcasses lining the rails, birds pecked and sucked at remaining afterbirth. The infant's skin sparkled to the rising sun reflecting off bloated insects. Overnight rains had rinsed the mother's scent from the gravel and railroad ties, leaving the child without a single trail to follow, without a single strain of familiar air to feed its fading breath.

Jack scooped up the body with a shovel he reserved for roadkill. He named the body

Ernie and called his boss to request leave for the remaining day.

The surgeon met with Jack to discuss options while Ernie lay in a room many floors away, kept alive by pumps and tubes and the hands of awestruck nurses. Both men folded and rested their hands atop the surgeon's oak desk, poised like opposite ends of a business negotiation. Ernie hadn't a hairline yet, so the surgeon agreed to cut and sew where he thought hair might grow. He sketched his plan with a green marker on a whiteboard propped beside the desk. The infant's head formed at strange angles, and the mother's apparently hasty drop-off only deepened the crevices, molded the already shifted bones to the difficult shape of rocks and metal tracks. Aesthetics meant little to Jack—his own grooming kit included one razor, a broken toothbrush, and a cracked mirror—so he told the surgeon, "I don't care how the hair grows. You're fine to just keep the brain in there however you can. Though honestly," and he leaned close, breaching the desk's perimeter with his large, hooked nose, "what are the chances it will ever work again anyway?"

The surgeon capped his marker. He shuffled through photographs taken upon Ernie's arrival. He rotated particularly strange images, searching to orientate himself to the correct angles among so much realigned skin. He let a long sigh ruffle stray hairs from his mustache. "I'll try to rebuild the brain back, but more importantly I'll try to just keep it in there." The doctor stayed with the photos. He stretched the sigh further. "I know you, Jack. You get paid by the carcass, and you're not the type to prioritize species. Why did you keep this one?"

"I think it's mine," Jack said. "Can't you see the resemblance?" He smiled for the doctor.

Hours later Jack occupied an emergency room waiting area with a family of three: one father, two daughters. Between failed attempts to quiet the giggling girls, the father dabbed his wet cheeks with a napkin. Jack met his glassy eyes twice, retreating quickly both times to his own projected pain. The girls played tag until one stubbed her toe. Only then did she join her father's tears.

After the surgery, the doctor pulled Jack from the waiting room back to his office. "I've never seen anything like it," the doctor said. "My team swears it too, that he should have died. We laid him out, went through the motions, we basically prepared for a loss. But that sound, the heart monitor, each beep would fuel another, and so on..." Each beep-beep, the doctor said, encouraged the boy's heart to further share the rhythm.

Jack smiled past every superfluous word. "I have a son," he said.

⌘

Jack's home rests at the intersection of a strip of railroad he adopted fifteen years ago and a woody area known for spewing wildlife into the town's suburban crawl. He enjoys watching from his window, the animals' adolescent pilgrimages from birthplace to a home of their own. But often the passages end interrupted. The years have trained Jack's ears to recognize the subtle thump of an animal cut short over the thundering locomotive beat. Utility bills and rent have their ways of changing the ear's physiology. The night Ernie dropped to the earth, that subtle thump against the ground woke Jack from dream in which he cared for a child of his own. He cleared his head of the dream and stepped out into the dewy morning, still feeling the imagined child's hand in his. "His name was right there on my lips," he says to the empty field at his front door.

Anticipating no more than a single doe, perhaps a family of raccoons if he were lucky, Jack idled his rusty Ford the short distance to the tracks, letting the image of a son of his own stew in his head. He closed his eyes, let the muscle memory developed by years of traveling this same path steer his truck.

He saw first a foot, recognized from his dream. The leg cascaded down the gravel bank, ending at toes the size of infected mosquito bites. Jack accepted the child's limp body not as a professional token, but as a realization of the night's vision.

⌘

Home from the hospital, Jack lays Ernie upon the worn living room carpet. Twisted yarns cradle the tiny body, nesting the way weeds and rubbish did just weeks earlier. Unhappy to let the floor have his child, the new father himself builds comfort; he experiments with blankets of various textures and densities, settling on a half-complete afghan that a dead aunt willed to him during her final stages of dementia. The blanket dangles unraveled at one end, but otherwise suits the baby and his bandages. Ernie's chest pulses to the irregular soundscape of cricket songs and croaking frogs. Jack watches his son survive through the night.

The night's rhythm breaks with the day. As the sun quiets the crickets and frogs, Ernie quiets too, the faint rise and fall of his afghan slows to a scarcely perceptible blip. Jack, already attuned to the breath of this child, wakes by the silence, jumps from the floor beside the boy, and panics. The blanket soon stops beating. Ernie's lips blue. Forfeiting the moment, Jack considers the shovel in his truck. "At least you were real for a day," he says to the body.

A train whistles in the distance. Its wheels grind a familiar click-clack, click-clack, and with that click-clack little Ernie's lip gathers crimson back, click-clack, click-clack. His valve flaps, whip-whap, then Jack picks at the limp wrap, unrolls the child and holds him close, afraid for what the passing train will leave as the click-clack inevitably dies to silence. Jack wills his own heart to pulse with the rhythm of the train. "Stay with me," he tells the boy. The new father forces himself into a panic, imagining the worst for his boy, the worst for himself, a life as it was just weeks before, more pulling the dead from the ground without this chance to place the living upon it. He imagines the worst so to fool his body into anxiety, to keep his heart feeding the boy long after the passing train.

As the locomotive whistle grows and the click-clack rattles Jack's window glass and dusts the carpet with abandoned cobwebs and ancient ceiling paint flakes, Jack pulls the boy tighter. The sound drowns even their shared beats. The whistle eventually passes, fades, Jack can hear his own heartbeat still drumming from within. He envelopes the boy, coaxing him to transition to Jack's beat. Ernie opens his eyes for the first time. "Green," Jack says. "Just like me."

⌘

Ernie learns to walk. And soon after, takes to chasing trains. The engines' laborious and productive rumbles mocks Ernie's own skewed gait. Jack anchors his boy by granting him a shovel and brings him along to scrape fetid flesh from rocks and streets. Jack calls it the family business despite having no reason to fake pride in his work; Ernie's comprehension tops out at the awe of his own footsteps. Intangibles like pride and family loyalty offer no beat of their own, so are of no use to the boy.

Some say the boy chased his mother's heartbeat, that the trains' rumble pounded stronger than Jack's chest. These whispers, perhaps his own, never spoken outside his head, bring Jack nightly to tears, but still he stays close to the boy, charging the young heartbeat the way his mother never did.

Jack took to scattering his own collected dead animals along the track in hopes of keeping his boy occupied during passing trains. The boy's misaligned eyes would widened, his crooked smile stretched, his distressed shirt—a gift from his father's closet—would throb at the chest as trains approached. "Mom," Ernie said, six years old, his first word. The following morning, Jack rose early and started planting these bodies of his own.

Ernie scooped. He dumped. Jack retrieved the carcass and returned it to the ground. Ernie scooped. This was the new rhythm, but could sate Ernie only temporarily. The routine weakened Jack's aging body, but strengthened his son's. An unfair but inevitable transition. Jack couldn't fight the train forever.

Ernie learns to wake to night trains. Jack builds alarm systems from rope and antique brass bells to intercept his son's escape attempts. Years pass. Ernie's awkward gait muscles to a skip, matures to a gallop, finally qualifies as a legitimate sprint. "Mom," he said at age six. "I'm coming," he learns at eight. One night, shaken awake by a railed monolith, larger than Jack had ever seen, he chases his boy, but cannot compete with the mother's heartbeat. Jack manages a final goodbye, but the deafening click-clack steals even that.

Petty Injuries

His most violent injury was birth. No fault of his own, of course. If concerned with fault one might be more satisfied with what the balanced would call *petty* injuries; paper cuts, fork mishaps, those resulting from infatuation with and lack of knowledge regarding electrical outlets. Fortunately, for Sam's mother, fault and blame are neglected devices.

Fault and blame can be forgotten after three steep flights of stairs. Pregnant-lady-take-the-elevator kind of steep. I-said-elevator, holy-shit-she's-falling kind of steep. A-faked-relief-when-the-child-is-born, but-born-*special* kind of steep.

Sam's frame is shoddy. His crooked three pieces—feet, knees, torso—appear stacked by a drunken creator and seem to disobey balance with every step. "Spider legs," his mother calls them, struggle to keep his torso from touching the ground. His head rides the resistance, cocked deep on a hinge, his shoulder a pillow like, as the old saying goes, *he's got a few screws loose*. Limbs are last minute accessories, there only to make sense of the larger picture, to make him fit as best unfair parts can do.

⌘

At the top of the stairs, Sam knows about gravity. Although never completely at terms with the reasons behind walls, the floor, hand rails, he understands them and sees no reason to test their boundaries. But gravity, it's a boundary he can exploit.

Laughter sounds like laughter but Sam knows which side he is on. Sam tops out at understanding the simplest concepts, but he is conscious of friendship.

⌘

At school or home friendship is a fixed pairing based on money or a court ordered community service project. Petty Theft Nathan has earrings and smells like a foot. On Tuesdays and Thursdays Elaine comes from an organization up town and brings colored paper and small toys for Sam and small gift boxes for Sam's mother who hasn't smiled since Sam's most violent injury.

⌘

He knows this laughing boy laughs at him. Sam would run, hide like his mother has told him to do, but from the top of the stairs the world looks too far down to grasp. He understands depth and recognizes the potential for pain upon impact to the hard ground below—he remembers it from his most violent injury—so he stays far from the edge. But the boy laughs and Sam, more than he wants silence, wants a kindred.

Pushing the enemy down this large flight of stairs is a feat only in that Sam's hand-eye coordination has never been fair. Ethically, Sam is justified in creating a new friend.

When it's all over and the enemy's body no longer laughs, when it has stopped bouncing from step to step, Sam is pulled away by unfamiliar arms into the tightest hug recent memory allows. He cries when the ambulance siren gets loud and the lights move fast. A crowd gathers quickly and hovers with feigned contribution; not offering help, but only the open-arm gesture of help. The excitement, the wide eyes and gasps are all outside Sam, but inside, behind the crying, Sam stares down at this possibility of his first true friend, *special* now and bleeding from the head at the bottom of the stairs, just as Sam did at his most violent injury.

Legs Unwilling

Summer bakes the metal playground slide to ripples. Still, kids line up. Sadists, all of them. Lucky enough to choose pain. Max feels it every breath, unwanted.

Max was a painful birth, breech, with legs unwilling. He cried, a good sign, but the sound only fell, like a deflating balloon's stale air. The limp curve of his mouth framed the weak breath. He met monitors and clamps within that first exhale. I asked the doctor, *is he as bad as we thought?* The doctor moved too quickly to answer.

These years later on the playground, kids impatient for the slide climb his chair and harness, pretend he's a chained monster. They mistake his twitches and ticks for smiles. His seizures for laughs. And his costume—a stained and stressed denim lion made by his grandmother, before she moved three states away to a place with a worse climate—allows just such a misunderstanding.

I knew he wouldn't be the same as others: I had no morning sickness; he moved little; family didn't bother with gifts. When I gave him a name, my mother asked why. *Because I want to name something, Mom.* I wasn't meant to live either. Parents named me Tammie because that's what the nurse's name was. I had *Max* picked out for years. I tried learning from my own birth.

But he kept breathing. Doctors didn't understand it. Even I hadn't a clue. A mother should know her child's language. I've since resolved to basic interpretation: is he satisfied or no? Only lately, I've been asking the same question of myself.

Twelve children were abducted from this park last year. Thirty-four in the region. I live ninety miles away, but I pray the drive is worth it. We missed our monthly angiography for this trip. The doctors should be noticing our absence right about now.

⌘

A man with sharp-parted hair and pressed slacks takes the empty end of my bench. He offers popcorn. I accept and toss kernels to the ground for birds. He offers part of his sandwich, which I accept for myself. He wears a predator's cliché overcoat, but doesn't stink the way I'd thought they should.

"He looks so precious in that lion outfit. My boy was Spiderman for Halloween." He extracts a wallet from his pocket, shows pictures of a boy who knows how to smile.

This man doesn't want my child. "He doesn't know what Halloween is," I say. "The fur is the only texture that doesn't make him bleed."

The man folds his wallet and rewraps his sandwich. "What's wrong with him?"

"Are you going to take him or not?"

"What? Why would I take him?"

"The coat. The hair. I thought you were shopping."

The man pockets his sandwich and leaves to an empty bench across the park. He sits, but keeps an eye attuned my way.

Max's father was probably the frat boy who fucked me on a dare. I remember his loose jaw, the way it flapped, guided by so much alcohol. Max has the same way about him. They share eyes, too, always spinning and barely open. Afterward, he hi-fived his roommates, and I went back to the bar, unsatisfied. But the glow had already been planted.

⌘

Hours later, when Max and I are the only souls left, after the sun has arched overhead to hover at the horizon and cast long shadows out of the monkey bars and the deserted swing-set, a second man claims my bench. "Great evening, huh?" He sits close, despite the open seats all around. He smells of cat piss and sweat. His long coat looks well-used. Birds escape.

"It still might be," I say, optimistic of this new stranger, offering a few left-over corn kernels from the bench. "For the birds."

"For the birds, indeed," he says and laughs when he eventually notices my offered popcorn. "Of course, 'for the birds,'" and he takes a few pieces.

He points to Max, hanging in his harness, moved only by sporadic breezes. "That your boy?"

I nod.

"I had a similar situation once. Some complications with surgeries ultimately killed him. But he was a drain, to tell you the truth. I don't mind saying it." He eyes Max, defiant against the sun's sharp reflections.

I squint, but still see envy in this potential taker. "I'd do anything for Max. No amount of money could keep him away from me."

He turns from the sun, my way, shakes his head slowly. "I'm sorry. I wasn't meaning to imply anything with your situation."

"I mean, if something happened to him, I'd give any amount to have him back."

The man's eyes widen. "Of course." He tosses a greasy kernel to the ground, no birds in sight.

"Your boy doesn't move much, does he?" The man steers my gaze toward Max and comments that he looks too still to be breathing.

"He gets tired easy," I say.

The stranger tosses a few kernels further than the last, almost reaching Max.

"Do you want him?" I scan the park's borders on the ruse of a stiff neck, searching for a van.

He creases his brow, ponders. "Do I envy your position, you mean? No, definitely not. I respect your fight, though." He throws the rest of his kernels. Some ting against the metal framework of Max's harness. Some bounce against his skin. He doesn't twitch.

No van. The sun dips lower, stretches the shadows long and thin along the ground. Max's silhouette creeps, edging my toes. "Your boy was a drain, huh?"

Out of kernels, the man reaches for a wood chip. "There was nothing left of my wife and I with him around. Max. His name was Max, too. It took both of us, two lives, to keep his one life going. Half-life, really. It sounds terrible, but that's the truth. I wondered how babies like him are even born."

"A kid like him makes it tough to believe Darwin, for sure," I say.

"You're religious?"

"I can't really believe in God either, can I?"

"I know exactly what you mean." He tosses the woodchip at Max, sighs when my boy doesn't respond.

"He's tired," I say. I check the man's profile against the dying light. His initially rigid features have softened, and even the stink has settled among the natural ambience. "I'll be honest. I was hoping you were a kidnapper."

The man smiles. "I am."

A bird lands within drooling distance of Max. My boy doesn't respond. His shadow blankets my entire foot, creeping to my knee. I shift away from the shadow, but can't shake the dark completely. "Did you take all twelve of them?"

He frowns. "Only five," and stands, wincing as his joints pop and echo against bench's metal back.

"None of them paid enough for you to stop?"

"I don't do it for the ransom." He buttons his coat, scratches his cheek. "I don't think of me as a selfish person. I imagine that nobody comes to a park with a known streak of kidnappings at this time of the evening—especially alone—without secretly hoping."

As the man turns from me, his stink resurfaces. I speak without breathing: "I don't–"

"Do me a favor and wait a half hour or so to call the police. Tell them you couldn't find a phone."

Already, and I don't dismiss the relief, I wonder what to do with his clamps and tubes and pills and van attachments; it's my space now. "What will you do with him?"

"I take him off your shoulders." The man approaches Max's harness, doesn't check for brakes on the wheels, and begins pushing him toward a dim parking lot. "Say 'goodbye' Max." Max only rocks to the pavement's pebbles and imperfections.

His shadow leaves with him. I whisper my own 'goodbye,' and sacrifice a single heartbeat for his absence.

Formaldehyde

William moved his fiancée to Brackenwood just months ago citing its high death rate as promise to a more lucrative life for him, her, and their impending child. He removes stains for a living, those left by dead bodies. When a heart stops, his wife gets cable for another month.

He'd thought the cleaning chemicals had made him sterile. Hoped, really. They can't afford a child. They visited a financial planner, their old neighbor, Gary, who invests mostly in aluminum cans and glass bottle deposits. "Think about it this way, for every baby that gets thrown off a balcony and you get called in to clean it, that's a month of diapers for yours." William didn't want to think about it that way.

The phenyl under his fingernails, pressed into his fingerprint crevasses warps every bite of food into fire. Fingerprints develop within the first twenty-four weeks of pregnancy, he's read.

The olfactory lobes—the scent glands—form as early as six weeks. He didn't know any of this until week ten when Julie finally revealed her pregnancy. By that time he'd already been inadvertently bathing the fetus in cleaning vapors, ammonia, too much peroxide, fumes he'd neglect washing from his clothes, letting them contaminate the air, fall into Julie's mouth, down her throat, and into the amniotic fluid flowing through the fetus's oral and nasal cavities. Scientists used to believe that smell depended on access to air. Now they could blame William should anything happen, could blame the bodies he cleans from the road as the source of his child's any imperfections.

He's read every book available at the modest Brackenwood library, searching for a possible loophole, a reason to believe that this child will be the one to outlive the trauma of a human lifespan. So far, nothing. The librarian, a hunched twig named Margaret, keeps the telephone near to her when William comes. She's taken to hiding the parenting books.

William arrives home, sweat, phenyl, and blood claiming his pores. Julie pushes William's hands back, tells him to wash with hot water before getting near her stomach. "The fumes could change it," she says. "Could take years off its life."

He read in one of the parenting books that infants crave touch, that the sensation of new skin to the surviving skin of a middle-aged father does something to an infant, *like a formaldehyde high might,* he thinks, *when cleaning out a burned building.* The book mentioned endorphins specifically, but formaldehyde, *nothing calms the way breathing a biological preservative can.*

With each phenyl breath William wishes the inhaled fumes *were* formaldehyde, solidifying his insides, making him capable of just a few more years, a reason to think he could mutate his genes to give any children a few more days than God could.

"How was work?" Julie asks, though only because their therapist, an old neighbor, Mauve, who tends to cats and head lice almost exclusively, said communication was important. He won't tell her about the man, baked to his kitchen floor, dead for days by the hottest Brackenwood summer on record, his leathered skin and the stink that goes with it. And the baby, unattended during the same sticky days, just ten feet away. Instead, he'll say, "We've got cable for another month and diapers enough keep our boy going for at least a few weeks," because there are so many people in this world, most of them destined for a perverted version of greatness.

Section Two: Aorta

Born Again Michael

Michael asks about my scars again. He won't give up. I fend off his questions between those from customers, bookending the feeding habits of corn snakes and the signs of pregnancy in guinea pigs with lies, lies, and lies. "War wounds," I've told him, but then he asks "what war?" "Allergic reaction," I've said, but then he offers Benadryl from his front pocket. I shouldn't let a pill-toting 8 year old boy loiter in my store, but then again I know where he gets those pill-toting habits. This store is a better home than he's ever had.

"Thank you," I tell the woman at the counter as she drops change into her purse. History: she drinks too much, sometimes settles for wells sludge just because she has too—kids to feed, and all that. Too often she buys cat food in bulk. Thing is, she owns a dog.

I look down to Michael. He's pulled one of the feeder mice from its cage and tip-toes en-route the boa against the far wall. I keep the constrictor's aquarium in the center of a wall, otherwise full of cavy and rodent homes. I'm sadistic like that. "Put it back," I tell him, then, "when I was a boy I was attacked by small, white mice," pointing to my scars. "They look harmless, but watch out."

"I've got band-aids too," Michael says and pulls a handful from his pocket with his free hand.

History: Michael has crammed the life of a 40 year old into his 8 year frame. His mother lactated ketamine, drowned his corn flakes in bourbon, and where other mothers christened kindergarten lunchbox napkins with *I Love You*s, Michael's sent reminders to lift cigarettes from the 7-11 on his way home from school.

"Let me feed him one," Michael says, pinching the feeder mouse by its tail.

"He already ate," I say.

"Half then," the boys says and separates the feeder's head from its body with nonchalant ease, as though he were sharing a candy bar.

"Christ," I say and move quick to dodge the erupting blood. I usher Michael quick behind the counter to keep the blood from the eyes of customers. The halved mouse is a feeder, yes, but unprovoked killing doesn't keep my cash register full. Already customers have left the store, leaving horrified gasps and a few gagging fits in their wake. "Come back," I plea. "The baby snakes can only eat half an adult mouse anyway," but they are already gone, and the bell above my door has already calmed.

One man remains, a tall, pale specimen who approaches the counter with all attention rapt by the blood now running over the floor from behind the counter. As the man sets a bag of Timothy hay and a ten-dollar bill on the counter, I hand a wad of paper towels down to Michael. "Kids," I say to the man, and shrug my shoulders like we've all been there, we've all beheaded a mouse with our bare hands. The pump from the feeder's still-beating heart matches my own heightened pulse.

"Blood doesn't bother me," the man says, his voice unnaturally monotone, like a flat-lined EKG. "In fact, I sorta enjoy seeing it flow. It's like a memento mori, you know?"

I do. Very much. Twenty years ago I was a boy who couldn't stand the sight of blood. That kid who wins science fairs and faints when forced in front of crowds, that was me. Nineteen years ago, a neighbor sliced his wrists with a canned corn lid. I walked in just as he cut. He spun around, painting his walls and floor and my face in red. I tasted the rust and copper of his blood, absorbed the panic in his eyes. Now, new blood literally means life to me. That taste changed me.

This man, I search for a wink, any sort of knowing gesture. But I come away with nothing atypical. History: he's a simple man who speaks in riddles. Born middle class. Will likely die middle class. His Bela Lugosi appearance serves as the only spike in an otherwise average life.

"Not sure I follow, sir," and offer his change and receipt with my free hand. With the other, I hold the feeder body below the counter and let the blood pool in my palm, careful to retain as much as possible in my hand.

"Just keeps me thinking about life when I see other things die, is all." He thanks me and steps out onto the cool evening air.

I turn back to Michael. He's abandoned cleaning the mess in favor of dragging designs through it with the towel. "It's the ocean," he says, gesturing toward three hieroglyphic waves rubbed into the blood.

I give him a bottle of Virex TB from behind the counter and tell him to clean everything before the stain sets. "I'm going to grab a bag from the back. Don't leave." I don't need this last command. He won't leave. History: when he's home, his mother throws needles at him like darts.

I step into the back of the store, the mouse body now floating in a palm-ful of its own blood. As soon as the door shuts, I have the body over my mouth, wringing it like a sponge. Drain cleaner, the way the everything just dissolves and washes away. Truly everything, I forget my own name for a moment with each swallow. There's heaven in ignorance like that.

History: those nineteen years ago, when I interrupted my suicidal neighbor, the moment I tasted his blood, I was changed. Seriously changed. Like seeing-tits-for-the-first-time changed. I don't use the 'V' word, but really what am I? I've never seen a pair of fangs, the sun doesn't cook me, I can't fly, but I do crave. The best I can understand is that when violence meets the taste of blood, synapses reroute. It's nicotine, really. Alcohol. I drink like anyone drinks—to forget. When my need to forget compounds, I'm left with an addiction.

What's to forget? Since tasting the suicide, I've been in touch with a hidden world perspective. Christian fanatics call it compassion. Social theorists would call it a form of collective consciousness. Hippies would call it "free love" or some shit. I call it mild torture. When I meet a person, I *know* their history. When I taste them, I *feel* their history.

Therein lays the conflict. Naturally, not everyone has a history worth feeling. For the first few years, I started fights on the schoolyard playground. Most of the empathy that came with those cuts and abrasions was standard grade school fare. I felt the history of kids beaten at home, a few kids molested, but mostly I tasted what I already had: a fear of teachers and cooties.

In high school I part-timed at a nursing home and skimmed from blood tests. During my short three years time, I swallowed hell. I learned that between drinks, I could purge the crippling empathy with a journal. This was an old Junior High trick my school counselor taught me when I sought his guidance during a devastating few weeks in which I *felt* that 1) my neighbor beat-off through binoculars aimed at my mother; 2) his son beat off to pictures of his own mother; and 3) my mother knew both of these things, and imagined them when she…you know. The counselor referred to my desire for blood as a "childhood phase." He blamed the

Blade trilogy. "Get your feelings out on paper; you'll feel better," he told me. It worked for a while...

19 July

This depression-era, black lunged racist named Edgar had me help with his diabetes testing today. One taste I took. One. Racist for a reason really, back in some hometown of his he tries to forget, a group of Mexican dealers fucked his sister, tied him to a tree and forced his eyes open with dinner forks. Kept yelling, something in Spanish, real hate in these faces. He cried when they did it. Punishment was all it was. Turns out, Edgar did nothing. Wrong guy. His sister didn't live through the hospital stay. Lucky I say. Feels good to get this out.

25 July

We got this transfer case named Aggie come in today, swollen and rocking like a damn waterbed. I hadn't drank anything since the Mexican history, so this lady, harmless looking enough, gets wheeled in and my mouth waters. Don't know what she had, if anything, but I tell her "routine blood test" and fill two needles. This poor fucker needs to pray for death. My own ass hurts after feeling what she lived through. Rape yes, but with dicks and objects, sometimes simultaneously. From her father, her uncle, a neighbor. They took bets on the number of beer cans they could hide. Told her they'd stand her on her head and use her as a koozie. I never drank the second needle.

...but I decided to downgrade to mice. Animal instinct is much easier to swallow than human emotion. Morally neutral animal blood doesn't have the lasting effect that human blood does, with its subtle complexities and nuances and—listen to me, I'm a fucking wine snob. Water vs. beer, really. One keeps you going. The other keeps you going in a much more satisfying way. But even though animal solace is temporary, it's still solace. So chin up and let the drug have its way with me.

"What are you doing?" Michael stands in the doorway.

"Christ, kid," I say, and shift the feeder quickly to my side, feigning nonchalance, like eating nothing more than a candy bar. "Ease up on the surprises." If I didn't know better, I'd say he, with this fucking Hollywood movie stealth, was the _ampire.

"Do you need this?" he says, holding out the Virex TB. He points to my chin.

"No," I say, and lick my lips. I drop the feeder into a bucket on the ground.

"What were you doing?" he asks again.

I wipe the remaining blood from my mouth with the back of my hand. "Let me show you something," I say, and lead Michael back out to the sales floor. When he isn't looking, I lick the blood from my hand.

Two new customers have wander in, a mother and daughter with matching enormous bee sting lips. They engage a sleeping puppy locked in a kennel. History: truly happy, these two. These are humans I could bleed without the adverse effects. "Can I eat you?" I ask them, quickly recover with "help you," but they are already out the door.

I usher Michael to a glass cage along the wall opposite the snakes. Inside, a Chilean rose tarantula cowers in the corner. "This is Maurice," I say.

"I know Maurice," Michael says. He smiles and taps the glass.

"Maurice doesn't eat food like you and m—...like you. Instead, he drinks the insides."

Michael nods, never pulling his eyes from the spider.

"Like apple juice. A person can either eat an apple or squeeze it to drink the juice inside. Let me show you." I open a drawer beneath the enclosure and pull out a single cricket. I drop the cricket into Maurice's pen. "Watch," I say to Michael.

Maurice immediately senses the meal and skitters to the front of the enclosure. Within seconds, he bites. Michael watches. "What's he doing?"

"He's doing what I was doing when you saw me with the mouse. Sometimes, the best part of something is the inside." I could turn this into an after school special, sell it for real blood money. *Skin color doesn't matter, little boy; we're all red on the inside.*

Michael watches Maurice slurp the cricket to a hollow carcass. "So," he says, stepping back from the glass, "you're a spider?"

I look up; the evening has turned to night. Traffic has slowed to a sporadic headlight. "Pretty much," I say and pull him away from the enclosure. "Get your jacket. I'm driving you home."

"I don't know. Last time my mom didn't like it."

"I know. But I'm not going to let you walk home in the dark. I'll talk to your mom if she gets upset."

History: Michael has reason to fear his mother. I pray, for the entire ride to Michael's house, that his mother isn't home. I pray that she's, at least, passed out. The engine revs to Michael's anxious pulse as we near the home, enter the street, and idle into the driveway, headlights off. "You can just drop me off. I think she's asleep, anyway."

"Let's make sure she is," I say and unlock our doors.

We're tiptoeing through the living room, our hearts calming, when the light comes on. For a second we're caught in this guerilla delivery. She's been waiting for us. Another myth destroyed: _ampire's can't see in the dark. Or perhaps just not my species. The *Scaredus Shitless*. Known natural enemies: boogey-men and vice-addicted mothers.

Adrenaline makes me thirsty.

"Where the fuck have you been?" she says to Michael, a drink in her hand. Something stained red with tomato juice, maybe too much grenadine. The drink sways at the end of a frail arm, thinned to bone with divots pocked throughout the flesh. Needle divots, fist divots, scarred mouth-sized divots. She disregards me.

"Ted's store," he mutters.

"Later..." she begins, a finger waving in his face, but the thought drops as she looks to me and steers her finger to my face. "He's home safe and sound. You can get going now." She takes a sip from her drink.

I look down to Michael. He's pissed himself.

"I'll stay around for a while," I say and push aside a stack of magazines on an oak end table. I sit. "Michael hangs around my store a lot. Maybe you and I should get to know each other."

Michael's mother takes another sip. Condensation drips from her glass, colored red by the liquid inside. I cough and pull my attention away from the blood with thoughts of baseball and nude grandmothers.

"I'm open to getting to know one another," she says, sliding next to me. Her thin frame finds plenty of room on the table next to me, despite my subverted attempt to take up as much space as possible. "I'm Mary." She licks her lips. The veins under her tongue pulse to the rhythm of my own beating organs. This close up, I can see a soft peppering of white powder under her nose.

"About Michael," I say, leaning back as she advances. "Since he and I are around each other quite often..."

Maybe it's the gravity but the final capillary levy somewhere in her head breaks free and blood pours. She's sipping from her drink and doesn't notice the beautiful cocktail being mixed, literally right under her nose. "Let me get you a drink," she says. She takes a large gulp of her own, "and a new one for me." She sets her glass, the cubes stained crimson, between my legs on the table.

"Go get a change of pants and a toothbrush," I say to Michael, who hasn't moved since we arrived. "Go out back and meet me at my car."

He's gone when his mother comes back. "Where's the kid?" she says.

"Bathroom," I say.

"Toast," she says and hands me a glass, fumes so thick the air around it moves.

"I've got my own," I say and hold up her discarded *Bloody Mary*.

I shouldn't. I know this woman. I don't need to *feel* her. But addicts, we don't live on logic; we live on sustenance. Her blood feels like sex.

I pull the glass from my lips, muscles numb from my mouth down my throat through to my fingertips and toes. I hold the glass by its rim and rattle the ice cubes. "I could go for another," I say. She smiles, says "me too" and turns toward the kitchen. Once she's out of sight, I run through the front door, out to my car, and meet Michael. "Get in," I say.

It's not until his house dips below the rearview horizon that Michael asks where we are going. "Crazy," I tell him, and smile until he does.

These are beautiful moments. Fresh with drink, the world succumbs to my perceptions.

The road guides me, the radio harmonizes with my pulse, the darkness outside doesn't hinder; it protects from traumas unseen. I've been high before. This is high*er*.

"You'll be okay," I tell Michael. "You're going to stay with me tonight, alright?" I search my gums for residual blood.

"Did my mom say it was okay?"

"I didn't ask."

"Take me back," he says. "She's going to be really mad."

"I can't," I say and already, too early, the mother's history begins to swell. The road throws me, the radio emits dissonant static, the darkness hides cruel purpose. I'm a young Mary, cornered…

"Really," Michael says. "She doesn't like it when I'm gone."

…Cornered and crying. My gut writhes, turning against itself, starved, reduced to tear away at its own tissue. "You're not going back tonight." I'm coughing the words and straining to keep the black road in front of me.

"What are you going to tell her?" Michael says. "She doesn't like being alone."

And I know why. Why she fights to keep her son close. Why it means beating him, to keep him scared to leave. Why it means cutting him if it's the last option she sees. The boy, he's a blanket, a shelter. He's a dog on a chain, bred and beaten to keep its owner secure. "I'll tell her...I'll tell her something."

Michael continues to beg retreat. His cries die to murmurs at the back of my skull. I can feel him listening for the voice of his mother hidden in the radio static, the wind outside the car, the throttled engine translated as her slurred demands. He's afraid of his mother's wrath. He's afraid of a life without it.

I'm a Mary alone for months. Parents gone. I can read the evening's journal purge already...

October 12th
Michael's mother lost her parents to a car wreck when she was young, too young to know that death meant fending for herself.

Family was a reclusive group, country home, distant neighbors, and an extinguished farm light. She tried praying, but even God didn't know she was alone. No friends came. No friends existed. She ate crumbs, but those lasted only days. Body breaks down after too long with no food. It eats itself, first digesting expendable tissues, then muscle, and finally, when you're an abandoned little girl with no family or friends, no one that even knows you exist, your body steals nutrition from the brain. The first lobe to go: the moral center. Cannibalism. Self. Nerves are dead so she can't feel the flesh tear from her arm. She takes the sight of her blood like spilled juice...

As we roll to a stop in front of my building, I'm still itching, but they are controlled urges. I have to carry Michael up the stairs, practically tie him to the couch. But eventually, he calms. I, on the other hand, continue to vibrate.

...The boy split her malnourished frame, even those years later, after medication, hospitalization, therapy, she stayed frail. The boy came suddenly, unplanned, an unprovoked attack from a guy she smiled at in a grocery store cereal aisle. She tried to get rid of him. Alcohol. Needles. Basement set-ups where guys with coat hangers traded elbow grease for a few grams. But he came. He tore through his mother. Mary bled.

Michael, he's settled, though floating on couch cushions saturated by his own sweat and urine. I'll clean them in the morning. Until then, he needs to know that a night of sleep doesn't have to be met with a morning of iodine and band-aids. I turn back to the journal.

"What are you writing?"

"Christ." He's over my shoulder. I close the journal and fend his question with bullshit. "Recipes."

"I can't sleep," he says.

"Probably because you're standing," I say, but shake away the joke and ask, likely the first sincere concern he's ever heard, "why?"

He shrugs. "I think I'll die if I fall asleep."

The words flow too smoothly. A boy his age shouldn't know how to piece together such a statement. "That's not true."

"But I want to," he says. "I want to fall asleep forever."

Nineteen years ago, when I walked in on my neighbor, when he sliced his wrist and bathed me with his blood, I was, myself, a beaten bag of frayed nerves and short circuits. That's how I knew my neighbor. Eight year-old me and this middle-aged product of divorce, jail time, court cases, bankruptcy, all the shit that muddles an otherwise promising head, we happened upon kindred depression one day when I brought his dead dog to his door. I had seen them walking together in the mornings. Then I saw the missing dog posters. When I found the animal, days later, flies already feasting, I brought the dog to him. Said I was sad for him. We became friends by communal misery. I wasn't friend enough to keep him from suicide, though. But his blood, I tasted it, and fell into its relief. I found my drug.

"You don't want to do that Michael."

"Yes, I do."

_ampires are just suicidals who have found their drug. Some people succumb to the burdens of the world, never knowing that imbibing the history of someone else may be all the fix they need. My neighbor, if only he'd tasted blood, may never have taken his life.

"I'll sleep on the floor next to you for tonight," I say. "If you feel the same way in the morning, we'll talk about it."

He nods. I walk him back to the couch, cocoon him within blankets, and tell him, "I'll put some water on the end table for you. There's a lamp if you need it."

He's already fighting the pull of his eyelids.

I set a glass of feeder blood, tell him it's juice, along with my open journal, spread to some of the worst pages, on the table next to him, inviting him to read. Violence and the taste of blood. It's this or suicide, and Michael has too much potential to waste it on death.

It Sparks

You never thanked me.

Should I have?

For your childhood, you should.

Thanks, then.

Don't be an ass. Not in front of your kid.

Thank you for my displaced childhood. I'm lucky
to have survived it.

You're welcome.

Fuck these modern tents. No character.

You, or the tents?

I remember your tents, dad. These look just like
them. Yours were smaller maybe, that's all.

Better. Mine had a history. Things brewed in
those tents. You included. You should thank me.

Then things change.

Then things changed.

Just give me a lighter.

If you planned on smoking, why didn't you bring a lighter, dad?

Don't end statements with 'dad.' It's rude, son.

Here. It sparks. Careful. Your oxygen.

...

..

....

When I was in the ring, I had the decency to place a few fans. You can't have your crowd sweating.

It's all hot air anyway. Use my sleeve, you're dripping.

This isn't a crowd. This is a fucking joke. What they need is a good scar.

Scare?

Either one.

Don't ruin this for Sam, okay.

Sam's fine. You're fine, right Sam? Pay attention to your grandfather when he's talking to you.

Dad. Don't.

I don't know where you got it. I never let you act that way around my father.

Your father died before I was born.

Lucky him.

......

...

....

At least blow the smoke away from us? And distance your tank some. This place is full of dry straw.

I'm not gonna blow it at the acts. Those animals are working. What are you doing?

Don't blame me for not wanting to follow in your failed footsteps.

They were good footsteps.

Drop it, please.

I suppose you got your own brand of animals in your line of work, huh.

Sure.

Can they be trained?

Dad.

Maybe you're the one being trained.

You flaunted an injury, dad. And you trained dogs. You had a barely-legal ring with a few misfit attractions and an audience eager to be conned.

I taught *you* to train dogs. Does that only mean something to me?

....

......

...

Who taught you to be ashamed of us? I want to know.

Society, dad.

They take everything from us, don't they?

But give us things in exchange. I'm lucky to have been hired. Those same laws that stopped your show are the laws that gave a carnie-kid a chance at a decent job.

God, I love that word. Carnie. People use to flock to that word.

Morbid curiosity governs most of us, dad.

Believe me, I know. Goddamn it's hot in here.

Sam, dad.

I'm out. Relight me.

You have the lighter. Careful. It sparks.

What about Sam? He could be an attraction. The Silent Boy.

Sam's fine.

What these people need…

….

…is some good ol' fashioned…

……..

…political incorrectness…

…

You shouldn't smoke in here.

This place is full of elephant shit.

I mean your health. Your oxygen.

The cigarette is medicine. Cancer is simply a side effect of a nicotine prescription.

…..

…

………..

These people are fine. They're enjoying themselves.

Think about how much I hurt to get my scar. The Lizard Man, they called me.

Now, you're a grafting patient.

These fucks could use a Lizard Man prescription.

Sam, dad.

You want to see this, don't you Sam?

Dad.

Hold this Sam. Careful. It sparks

COME ONE. COME ALL

Dad.

SEE THE LIZARD MAN. FORGET THE MERE PARLOR TRICKS AND TRAINED TRIVIALITIES OF THIS SO CALLED CIRCUS.

Sit dad.

THE PRODUCT OF AN AMAZONIAN MOTHER AND A HOBO FATHER. HE'S A PILE OF SCALES. A REPTILIAN WONDER. AND HE'S HERE, BEFORE YOUR EYES.

Careful, dad.

Take my tank, Sam. Keep it away from the cigarette. WITHOUT A DOUBT, A WONDER BEYOND COMPREHENSION.

And my shirt, Sam.

Dad.

RAISED IN THE ARIZONA DESERT, THE HEAT HIS ONLY FRIEND.

Grandpa…

TOUCH THE SKIN FOR A SMALL DOLLAR. TAKE A PICTURE FOR TWO. BRING HOME STORIES

FOR YOUR FAMILY, OF THE BURNED SKIN
LIZARD MAN

Grandpa, it's sparking…

Car Dodging

How the bald man with the needle in his median cubital vein said he found God felt like what a rape would be if afterwards the woman zipped up her pants, fastened her belt and said, "thank you, I've been so busy lately."

If I were to tell these people in these chairs giving blood that it's really a Russian roulette with the needle, that any could be hepatitis, HIV, syphilis, prostate cancer, and they shrug and say, "I have sick leave to use anyway"—that's what this man did to me.

I've seen traffic backed up for blocks sometimes, horns destroying any peace in the air. Fisticuffs. Verbal assaults. And this man, it's like he steps from his vehicle, leaving the car idle, and smiles to himself: "I can walk from here." A stalled car is useless to me, just like this bald man, high on his own story of revelation.

⌘

My day job doesn't stop at penetration. Even beyond the stick it's my job to calm, to reassure the donors that they are doing the right thing by giving blood so that the drunk driver in room 418, with his blood thinned to spilling, will be able to give the unfamiliar country road another shot, so that when a man is rushed to the emergency room after a failed attempt to rob a grocery store he doesn't have to die. He can get well and try again. Get right what he did not see through the first time. *It makes me feel good to give*, they say, *to bleed so that others can, too*.

I'm a cynic, sure, but that's what getting robbed will do to a person.

This man smells like he believes bathing is vain and starts by whispering to me, asking if I have ever experienced something I can't explain. Staring at his head I answer "patterned baldness."

He doesn't react. Having acknowledged the shine reflecting from the top of his head I'm drawn now, helpless, absorbed into the white light glare like from the revelations I've heard so many people speak of, that one moment when everything makes sense and what was just prior something a person would call customer hotlines about becomes understood as a simple human mistake. Finding a bone in a corndog becomes FDA acceptable. Fur on the surface of cottage cheese is just an epiphany to a healthy lifestyle free from dairy product fat. The donors, they just sit and talk as though revelation is listed just above bowel problems on an item sheet of appropriate conversational topics while giving blood. Just below family: children, husband, pets. When this bald man reaches over for my hand, grasping it with the nervous sweat my job says I am supposed to keep from flowing, I sit back and pull out the comic page from that morning's newspaper. I've heard all the revelations before. Nothing impresses anymore.

I've heard a man tell me God spoke to him through his Cheerios. "Now you're just forcing metaphor," I told him.

A woman, a nurse, once told me that God revealed Himself to her via the "natural human drive towards euthanasia;" that when a human being sees another in pain synaptic reflexes take over to end the suffering. We mistake the drive as compassion, but in truth we are only victims of a response designed as compassion. Thirteen dying-slash-dead patients later—and a house built on funds left to her in wills muttered through last breaths—finally allowed this woman to understand what the world was about. Love made sense, she said. "But you don't," I told her.

I shake the newspaper flat and wonder if today is the day Odie finally fights back. Or will Garfield again exploit his disposition toward canine gullibility?

The bald man began as all their visions do, with a common denominator. *A day like any other*, something with universal relevance: he was driving back from coffee for two at a late night diner. The arrangement was something he now acknowledges as premeditated, saying his boss threw the meeting together considering the crowded area as an appropriate venue to break the news of the bald man's termination from wherever it was he worked. Law office, accounting firm, daycare, I don't remember, but when he got to the part about driving during the night under the depressive influence of his uncertain future, when he said *something* shot across the road, I paused in the middle of the third panel in a new cartoon called Sleeping Dogs, and brought the newspaper to just under my eyes.

This bald man's face hung deep as he told his story. He broadened the intricacies in effort toward empathy. He wiped small beads of sweat from the bald curve of his forehead. With his hands he punched the air in quick, open-handed jabs, piercing words like 'brakes' and 'human shaped.' Then he mentioned other dark images he saw still in the ditch, hoping, he said, that they weren't already hurt. He said whatever it was that ran out in front of his car that night did something more than what "losing twenty pounds could ever do." "Almost hitting something," he said, "was like an electrical blackout just before the bomb goes off, you know what I mean?"

Yes. I knew exactly what he meant. What I had there in the chair before me was a cut brake line when I didn't plan on stopping anyway. A robbery.

⌘

See, the way it's supposed to go is that there's a point system. Back in juvy everything had a point system. Guards kept the morale as subdued as they could, but gentle competition had a way of sneaking into otherwise mundane activities. Working the cafeteria, I assigned myself a single point for every detainee's request for second helpings. Like I was an inside man, like I could fulfill such requests without being held accountable at the end of the day. I had long hair and depressed demeanor, and I guess that's all it takes sometimes to be approachable by misfits hunting for connections. After all, Icky and Justin, two co-detainee's, both had long hair, and that's all it took to get us talking. We were all three migrated to the blood center upon being let go from the county detention center following funding cutbacks. And all three shared a love for friendly competition. I think it was Icky's idea to dodge cars. His father was a NASCAR driver.

With the outside air humid enough to keep the mud on our faces from cracking, and the blades of grass that line shallow ditches pliable enough not to cut wrists or thighs, we get dressed for a game of car dodging. If the air holds enough moisture to keep windshield wipers steady it would seem insulting not to organize a game. Icky and Justin dress in deep red, something they learned from a book about ninjas, but I cover in all black. In the ditch we wait, whispering the faces we will make or jumps we will take, if we even choose to do so— a skip at the end or a stridden long jump style. With what we paste on our faces, mud and sometimes strips of old newspaper like papier-mâché skin grafting, whatever will catch any driver unaware, we wait for the one small speck of light in the distance to bounce off of the asphalt. That's what we see first.

The universal 'ready' position in car dodging.

As the cars near, the lights take shape in stages. First, just blurs of round white light, barely distinguishable as two separate units. Next, sharp and cross-shaped, separated by headlight mitosis.

It's the universal 'set' position in car dodging.

Then, round balls of glow just feet from our noses. The universal 'go.'

At 'go' one of us runs to the ditch at the other side of the road, fueled like the torque of a primed slingshot. We can feel the heat oozing through the grill. The sound of tires ripping water from the road booms through our bones the way a heart beat can be felt at these times, inches from the impact of this two ton bullet. From the ditch the players who aren't running cheer.

What I saw before this bald blood-doner and his new faith was three points to the player who gets closest to the car, two points for hang time if you decide on that jump at the end, and one point for every second the driver cautiously takes to reach the next intersection. I've scored twenty-four points in a single run once.

Now all I see is a life saver. My sharp silhouette flashing for a blink in front of a darkened windshield is nothing more than a savior. Mere rebirth. Midnight drivers aren't tired enough to wrap their car around trees anymore. They aren't drunk enough to bumper-tackle midnight joggers anymore.

Instant sobriety.

This bald man speaks of something that should be dead, something that should have made him dead. But for some divine reason it isn't dead. Marking the start of his rebirth was what I know as a simple game where points are no longer sufficient. What Icky, Justin, and I had was a self-help program at our expense.

"Oh, but don't feel left out," the bald man says, going for comfort. The donors do this often, feeling obligated to assure those of us not fortunate enough for a near-death experience that one day we will get our chance. He might ask my name and use it once. "You'll be a part of something so brilliant some day. Giving a pint or so when I can, for me, is just a way of giving to those who aren't where I am yet. Letting them live long enough to see what I have seen."

And I ask the man at the end of his testimony if he gets the humor in this week's Family Circus.

"What's your name, son?"

"James."

"It's supposed to be funny cute, James," he says, "not funny ha-ha."

"Of course," I tell him.

Of course. The humor is skewed, and this thief becomes clergy through car dodging. Of course. Heaven on accident through car dodging. Of course. Patterned baldness as underserved wisdom through car dodging. The man bites through a grin, all honor and humility as the sterilized needle siphons blood at a textbook rate, safe, unnoticed by the organs of his bloated body.

At the refreshments area a woman sits against the table stuffing sugar cookies with red icing into baggies. She breaks cereal bars into smaller squares and slides them into the deep corners of her purse. She times her grabs between the passing eyes of donors and employees alike.

"I'll be right back," I tell the man, patting my hand in faux comfort hard to his shoulder, giving a slight tug to the needle and its tender insertion point. I flick it a bit as I stand, wanting pain, but he stays undisturbed. "A magazine or anything?" I ask him. He doesn't move.

By the time I reach the refreshments table crumbs survive where once sat full cookies and crackers. A few slices of summer sausage and some hard candies are all that remain as proof of this woman's pilferage for sugar coated baked goods.

She notices me just as I walk up behind her. Her hair stands thin, shapes a perfect lollipop. I can see her scalp through its split end canopy and red tips the roots are trying to extinguish. She poses as a donor, but her subdued cunning belies any generosity.

"We're having a bake sale," she says calmly, pulling close to her purse, large enough to be a tote bag, "to benefit a missionary trip. That's why I need them."

"Those are for the donors," I say.

"We are going to speak about faith," she tries as though it were the great equalizer, as though faith heeds this sort of immunity. "You want to buy a brownie?" She asks me.

"The donors," I repeat.

"Fifty cents for two. I think they're real fudge, but I haven't tasted them yet."

"You're stealing," I say.

She waves a brownie in small circles under the brace of her elbow rested on her crossed legs. If the brownie were a cigarette, smoke rings would bellow from her mouth and her voice would have reason for its seduction. With the brownie she tries for a less subtle persuasiveness, chewing the corner of it, moaning just enough for implication.

"You can't just eat those without giving some blood," I insist.

"Let me give you something else then,'' she says in a voice switched to coy. She grabs the hem of her dress, threads hanging loose to the floor, and slowly lifts the cloth. It rises past her white socks, past her calves dotted with specks of black hair where large veins collide like streams of blue water hitting the rocks and boulders of a waterfall. I see four different shades of peach under just the first foot of her dress. "How much further are these brownies worth to you, sir?" She asks, and the would-be smoke rings float to my face, smashing against my nose and eyes.

Something with her saying *sir*, tells me to fuck the brownies.

The way watching buildings burn makes a person schedule a return visit the next day to see what he can find let me look into the promise of this situation.

I am an environmental activist pocketing aluminum cans for gas money.

I am a poacher helping the world of its rabid polar bear problem with the agenda for a new winter coat backing my hunt.

I force connection and stretch implication until a slight grin creeps from my face. "I guess just a little further," I say. In juvy this sort of opportunity is what we'd call a 'game ender.'

Her face turns. All of the come hither, now shrew in an instant. She drops the hem, keeps the brownie half in her mouth and stands. Eyes squinting and one finger aimed at the center of my forehead she says with all the sincerity of dissociative identity disorder, "I'm speaking of faith."

I am an animal shocked by the absurdity of headlights.

The woman turns her head as she walks past me, brushing the grain of her hair across my chest. She leaves the building, commanding the space around her, and like gathered troops a few donors turn. Some stay, still it seems deep into their own stories of revelation. The volunteers who do what I do, keeping the donors calm, feign interest. I bring my gaze back and look to the empty table, a few spots decorated with colored sprinkles or dabs of fallen icing, and I realize what the woman has gotten away with.

The bald man at my station waves me back over. He holds my discarded comics page. "Hey," he says already boiling a deep laugh, ready to cough, "Look at this Peanuts. Charlie Brown is trying to kick the football again. What a damn idiot."

It was time to take car dodging back.

⌘

Rallying the boys tonight is met with a couple slight complications. Justin, just last night, fell back into county detention by means his mother refuses to mention over the phone, outing him as a player. Icky, like his forgotten real name, has completely disappeared and nobody we know mutually feels it necessary to find him. That's Icky, excited about tomorrow one day and gone once tomorrow comes. But today, the day I need him most, he has vanished. I'm sure his disappearance coincides with Justin's, as the two routinely endured simultaneous punishments in juvy. It very well could have been a game whose rules I was never privy to.

It's just me, and suiting up as a single black form without the contrast of two in dark red comes with a flashing mutual understanding between me and the sparsely lit night: We are each there for what we need to get done. I, as black as the night would let me, and the night, giving reason for the headlights I hunt.

When walking the roads, waiting for a ditch to call, I measure distances by the focus of the yellow bulbs at the horizon. I judge turns by the reflection of the lights in sporadic house windows, darkened by the need for a night's sleep where the decisions of the day can carry over one more, and what was before can be on its way to forgotten. As the light bounces against mist-fueled puddles in the road I check the surroundings for a suitable spot from which to take back everything that had been taken away.

I've learned that believing in something causes a person to go distances in order to prove to themselves that what they have invested in isn't a complete waste of time. Like the revelations I've heard—the nurse forcing herself to discredit even the most promising medical advances just two blinks after she's overloaded a glycerin drip becomes pride over practice. I understand this by watching windshield wipers wave to me as the cars they protect speed by.

Offered help means only that the giver wants proof of validation. The hum of rubber against damp asphalt teaches me this.

I listen for reason in the steam from rain on hoods and tail pipes.

Staring at license plates as they near, I twist the letters into something I can read as supporting evidence.

Deep into the glow of headlights I search for an understanding to the way all of these lessons have come from a game with a point system. Does necessity breed epiphany?

With blackness stretching into vastness on either side of me I step back into a ditch, holding at its very bottom a stream of stale water. Breathing becomes conscious. I screen my breaths' quivers and tics into something smooth and quiet. I sink into context, a rock in a ditch, and I wait for something to happen. I wait to prove to the world that what I have is not a waste of time.

Fighting through the sting of iced feet I see one small speck of light in the distance.

The universal 'ready.'

I see the sharp crosses they become.

The universal 'set.'

Then I see the perfectly round balls of glow just feet from my nose.

The universal 'go.'

And without the cheers to my back I jump from the slick grass to the wet asphalt, my shoes sloshing wet noises under the crescendo of a throttled car engine. My lungs emptied of air. And I stop. I take a deep, principled fill of air and stand still, searching the windshield for a sign of give from the driver. Nothing. First, my knees buckle. As plastic cracks over my head a halo bulb of a blinding headlight covers my face like a fist. I smile through the pain and wait on the ground for a curious driver to come back, to see what he has done, to respond in the only way this situation should produce. No revelations, no reason to give back to lesser individuals, no theft of anything.

Just a dumb kid getting hit by a car.

But the car doesn't stop. It drives on until turning away down some distant street. Exhaust dissipates as my eyes blur. Blood cuddles close, a slowly growing puddle with whispers of remorse. The rain feeds the puddle, a pond to a lake to a sea, and finally to eddies and tributaries. My body drains and for the one moment I have I ask for a few pints from a stranger to let me believe a little longer.

Behind everything belief structures break down and form again to incorporate new factors.

Behind everything the road ends, a power outage three seconds to detonation.

Or maybe it doesn't, and I finally realize that if I need closure bad enough I will see it in anything.

Snake Girl at Scab

Lacy tells me to stop staring at the old man across the street. She tugs my sleeve and motions toward the waiter standing at our table. This is Scarab, our favorite Indian sidewalk café, my wife's and mine. We come here to cool down after arguments, and have agreed to keep this place sacred, to not ruin it with painful bickering and dinnertime condescension. I've named this place Scab, which feels more appropriate. "No menu for me, Francesco," I say. The waiter doesn't wear a name badge. We come here a lot.

We spent the day picking out lampshades. Not lamps. Lampshades. She had opinions informed by daytime home remodeling shows, and I apparently had an inconvenient lack of opinion. That landed us at Scab during Vineville's monthly art festival. We've come here before, sans the Band-Aid motivation, to take in the art. That's how we discovered Scab. We even held hands a few times. But as the home arguments intensified and the nights out decayed into sloppy patching sessions, we weren't left with much time to take in the beauty around us.

The old man, he has two wedding rings. One on his finger, the other, a diamond-topped elegant thing hanging around his neck. He paces by the booths, stopping every few steps to lean close into a painting. He inhales the color, lives inside the brush strokes. His favorites seem to be simple scenes with husbands, wives, and secrets. Every few booths an artist offers the old man a painting for a discount. The old man shakes his head, and with it the ring hanging from his neck.

Lacy tugs my sleeve. "I said, 'you aren't hungry?'"

"Sorry, hon." I look up to Francesco. "Just a coffee for me."

"No beer tonight, sir?" he asks. I wave him away.

"You're a million miles away tonight," Lacy says. Just an observation. Not an invitation to vent.

"Just thinking about lampshades," I lie.

"You know the rules, Eric."

The old man accepts a beer and a whispered joke from a skinny artist. The old man laughs. Maybe that space where his wife used to be isn't empty, but breathing room instead. "I've been thinking—" I say to Lacy.

"They haven't even offered any naan," she says, loud enough for Francesco to hear. I smile an apology to our wartime friend.

"When was the last time we looked at art together? When was the last time we shared something strange or shared some surprise?" I ask.

"What's with you?" she asks, craning her neck for visions of incoming Indian bread.

The old man shakes off a staccato chuckle, takes a sip of his beer, and turns from the booth. The sun has dropped, queuing streetlamps and shallow track lighting to illuminate the night. Beige pantsuits have been exchanged for knee length sundresses and bunned hair has escaped to ride the evening breezes upon naked shoulders. Somewhere a band spills sound. This is the time when the freaks come out, Lacy says. The old man nearly collides with barefoot young girl holding a thin snake. I listen for a comical clash of cymbals. Hear none, but chuckle anyway.

"You're acting weird," Lacy says.

The girl maintains a stern posture, a careful demeanor, almost a chemically supported daze upon her face. She speaks to the old man, her lips expressionless like she's warning him of something inevitable. Like *there's no use in trying to build a bomb shelter this late, but I thought I'd still tell you it was coming*. The old man listens with the flamboyant nod of a learned generation encouraging the learning generation. She holds up her snake. The old man waves her away. She turns from him, catches me staring at her. I lift my hand to my face, an awkward attempt to curtail accusations of voyeurism.

"Where's your ring?" Lacy says just as Francesco drops a basket of naan to our table.

"I left it at home."

Sometimes I go out on the weekends without my wedding ring. I'm not hunting for other women, but conversation tends to be so much simpler if they assume I am. Other times, I think, I forgo the ring as an invitation for misery.

She throws her knuckle in my face, her ring sparkling by the amber lights around us. "I always wear mine." Of course she does. She loves displaying gems enough to feign the sentiment behind them.

"Would you if there was no diamond?" I say, wanting to swallow back the words even as they flow, yet flow so naturally I will admit. She opens for rebuttal, but I tell her, "You know the rules."

She tears a piece of naan. "When you gave me this," she says and holds out her hand, palm down. "I was surprised then."

"I wasn't. I knew you'd fall in love with the diamond." I tear off a piece of naan for myself, but only roll it in my hand. The dry bread crumbles to the tabletop.

"When we saw that car wreck on I-5."

"I've seen wrecks."

"The miscarriage?"

The bread crumbles to nothing. "Somehow, no."

Lacy swallows, places her diamonded hand in her lap. "So are you saying we should—" She's interrupted by a tap on her shoulder. She jumps. I jump.

The barefoot girl with the snake stands at our table, a small gang of dark dressed boys riding her scent. The girl has an eggshell canvas for skin, spotted by harsh eye shadow, spackled blush, and pink lipstick the color of a newborn's nursery. She can't be older than twelve. "You want to touch it?"

Lacy and I take in each other's confusion, the implication of possibility seeding smiles.

"Won't it bite?" Lacy says.

"I don't think he understands his body," the barefoot girl says.

The snake writhes over the girl's palm, held back at the end by her skinny fingers, painted a red as fierce and young as the pink on her lips. The girl alternates her gaze between Lacy and me, never addressing the snake, never fearful of what it may do. She knows this snake, would be surprised by nothing. I sweat. Lacy sweats.

"What do you think, Eric?" Lacy says. "I wasn't expecting to touch a snake tonight."

"Me either," I say.

We reach for the animal, fingers extended ready to receive something unexpected.

The barefoot girl pulls back. "One dollar," she says.

"No," I say, the salesman in me instinctively stretching to bargain. The girl's face maintains her stoicism, a game really, knowing that one dollar isn't a livelihood for her, it's an excuse to play. "One dollar," she repeats.

Then what? A one-dollar patch to carry Lacy and I through to another Scab dinner. I wave the girl away. I don't wait for Lacy to see something special hidden in the strange barefoot girl and her strange snake and her strange gang of strange men. She'll find it, because she's afraid of a future without it. I can't waste a dollar on fake possibility. "So, I've been thinking," I begin again as Francesco pops up for a guerrilla coffee delivery, escaping just as quickly.

Norman Rockwell Nostalgia

CYCLES

Though he's not big like his father, tiny Brian knows how to break noses. His kid sister, a curious child with an unhealthy interest in tiny Brian's business, knows it now, too. Her doctors, too. The police are learning, and the neighbors have already selected sneers for any inevitable confrontation. Unfairly, his mother, who ran the father off after one too many of her own bruises and broken vessels, receives the heat; "bad parenting" and "oh my"s and all that. The neighbors retract party invites. Dad always said to hit back. But dad's gone the way of baited women and other wombs. So tiny Brian takes shots at his pillow for practice, just in time for his kid sister to interrupt. To Brian, his kid sister is less family than she is target practice. *But don't worry, mom. Dad taught me how to hit back, and I'll teach you.* This, from the hospital waiting room, while his kid sister suffers unaffordable operations to ensure she won't miss out on all the scents of childhood.

NORMAN ROCKWELL NOSTALGIA

In lieu of recess, tiny Brian sits alone with Mrs. Bellin in a classroom outfitted for nurtured optimism. Nowhere, office cubicle grey. Nowhere, the latex smell of nursing home corridors. Nowhere, prison steel sweat. Everywhere, colors, vivid unnaturals. This childhood dreamland frames perfect Mrs. Bellin at the front of her classroom, overlooking her delinquent tiny Brian as better children play outside. Behind Mrs. Bellin, a Norman Rockwell print of a boy, his father, and a bandaged knee. "Where is that?" tiny Brian asks.

"That's just a picture, Brian." Mrs. Bellin claimed a headache this morning, would rather sit quietly with tiny delinquents than govern children outdoors. She's had headaches a lot lately, ever since the used car lot had to close down, giving her husband rec time at home.

"But where is it. Where do they live?"

Honesty breeches Mrs. Bellin's tempered exterior. "Nowhere, Brian. It's good that you learn this now. That scene," she cranes toward the painting above her, bruised flesh revealed at her clavicle, "never happened."

Tiny Brian approaches his teacher, his own bruised clavicle forcing a wince at every step. Mrs. Bellin takes note. "If that were a picture of you and me," he tells her, "it probably wouldn't sell very well, huh?"

"Nobody would buy it, Brian."

LEARNING BEFORE CLASS

Lawsuits and an opinion-bloated public keep tiny Brian and Mrs. Bellin silent. But before school, on the ruse of tutoring hours, they commiserate on the origins of their wounds, happy to breathe and not worry of the repercussions.

Mrs. Bellin's husband strips away his amiable social veneer at night to accessorize his wife with welts and purple flesh, like eggplant leather exterior. "Hitting me only where nobody can see the marks," Mrs. Bellin says. Tiny Brian's father returns some nights, when his mother leaves for bar therapy among fellow domestic targets, to make sure his boy knows how to be a man. *Taking a few smacks is a manly thing to do.* His father surveys the refrigerator, leaves, promises to one day come back for good.

"Taking a few smacks is a manly thing to do," tiny Brian says to Mrs. Bellin.

Mrs. Bellin maneuvers a dulled pencil around a math equation. A teacher from down the hall passes her door, waves, says hi to her and tiny Brian, but doesn't wait for a response before moving along. "I don't think anyone should have to take any smacks," Mrs. Bellin says, adjusting her felled collar over the mountained purple clavicle below her neck.

"So why do you?" tiny Brian asks. He checks the equation on his homework. Nothing but hieroglyphics when set against the visceral language of a night spent winded and bleeding through his sheets.

Mrs. Bellin pulls the homework from his peripheral. She has a new assignment. "We're going to heal and be done with all of this." Tomorrow, they agree to celebrate wounds of their own creation.

Author Notes

Click-Clack

Click-Clack exemplifies what I try to do with a story. Simply put, that is to move a reader, to edge the reader as close to sickness as possible without losing my literary integrity, to be simultaneously grotesque and heartfelt. Okay, so not so simply put. I suppose that's why instead of writing a manifesto, I instead wrote Click-Clack.

This story materialized just after a lengthy bout of promotion for my novel *Stranger Will* and just as I finished the final edits for my novel *I Didn't Mean to be Kevin*. *Stranger Will*, a novel about a man wanting to distance himself from parenthood, *I Didn't Mean to be Kevin*, a novel about a boy wanting nothing more than to have a parent, beautifully bookends Click-Clack in theme and content. I believe this story was a response to having finally dusted my hands of those two novels, which were, at the time, the longest pieces of fiction I had written. I needed to purge those crannied demons. Click-Clack, though, I feel ultimately re-invigorated them.

I've perhaps had more direct feedback from Click-Clack than I have from any of my other stand-alone stories. A close second would be my very first published story, Petty Injuries. Though years stand between the two stories, they seem both of the same thematic egg.

Petty Injuries

Petty Injuries was the first piece of fiction I had published entirely on my own. By that I mean that no academic or professional connections made this Dogmatika publication possible. Yes, I had come to Dogmatika by way of other writers, and of course I made sure to mention those writers in my submission letter to Dogmatika, but those writers weren't my key to the editor's desk (at least I hope not; Christopher J. Dwyer, if you are reading this, tell me if I've been promoting a false sense of accomplishment all these years).

It's interesting to me how similar this story, my oldest piece of published fiction, is to my newest piece of published fiction (at the time of this writing, "Click-Clack"), in terms of content—deformed child, willing-but-unable parent, birth defects. Despite the years between the former and the latter—five—and despite the various thematic turns I've taken during those years, I've come back to the domestic grotesque. (This isn't a reflection on you, mom, I promise.) If anything, this goes to show me what a bit of positive feedback can do. Petty Injuries gave me some attention so, whether subconsciously or not, I continued to stretch the deformed child for years, until it became my own personal trope of sorts.

Legs Unwilling

If you are reading these stories, and these author notes, by order of the table of contents, you're likely sensing a pattern. What exactly draws me to the childhood grotesque? I've mentioned in interviews, and have had this notion reaffirmed by other writers (check the blurb from Tim Hall for *Charactered Pieces: stories*), that not ever having a stable paternal figure in my life might account for the reappearing unwilling parent character in my fiction. And if I can be my own couch therapist for a bit, perhaps the extent to which my unwilling parents actually become the sympathetic character says a lot about how I want to displace blame from my mother for my own fatherless childhood. I was young when she and my father divorced, too young to have any real opinions on the matter, so I exist now in a sort of genetic limbo, knowing the roots are there but never able to fully comprehend them. Fiction helps me understand my place. And if not understand it, at least digest it.

Legs Unwilling is an especially dark story as it not only brings into question a parent's desire, or ability, to care for a handicapped child, but also brings in a somewhat unexpected sympathetic character, the kidnapper. Though I've received less feedback on this story than on most others, the feedback I have received has been considerably more opinionated. I am fortunate enough not to have a child with physical disabilities, but if I did, honestly, I might pray for a kidnapper.

Formaldehyde

Formaldehyde, adapted from the first chapter of my novel *Stranger Will*, exemplifies the philosophy of the novel's protagonist, William Lowson, quite succinctly. In a way, William was me. At the time I began writing the novel, I had been dating my then girlfriend, now wife, for a while. She was the first girlfriend I ever had that talked openly about having children. Until that moment, perhaps guided by my own childhood, perhaps not, I wasn't interested in having children. *Stranger Will* is the result of me trying to intellectualize my feelings on the matter (intellectualizing having become my preferred mode of addressing new ideas since adopting my new university environment).

William's defense is to blame his occupation for his (overly?) rationalized view of parenthood. And though his argument, that being born means being dead eventually, makes logical sense, his character required more than nihilism to be empathetic. Enter Mrs. Rose, the devil on his shoulder, and her group of Strangers.

I've been questioned about my motivation for writing *Stranger Will*, and even more so now that I have a child of my own. I assure everyone, I love my child. As Freud might say, sometimes a cigar is just a cigar.

Born Again Michael

Born Again Michael grew out of peer pressure. Vampires were never a subject I cared much to write about. Many of the other contributors to the *Eternal Night* collection are writers I had been working with for years. One day, Christopher J. Dwyer approached this group of us with an opportunity he had been given: to collect and edit a group of vampire stories. I considered the invite a challenge.

Because I . didn't understand the conventions of vampire fiction, and I didn't want to risk the wrath of schooled readers by introducing something into the genre that might jar the reader at best, or completely turn the reader against me at worst, I instead created my own domesticized vampire origin story. As per usual, a child plays a central role.

Born Again Michael became a much better story than I imagined it would be. This story marks a point at which I learned to embrace the quick-witted first person perspective, something I've come back to over the years. My fiction, I am learning, generally takes one of two voices: 1) the quick-witted and 2) the grotesque and descriptive. Someday I'll find a way to merge the two styles. On that day,

I'll probably hate myself for forcing that which should not be forced.

It Sparks

Here is another story born of a challenge. Paul Eckert, editor of *Sideshow Fables*, started his literary journal with the goal of compiling stories that incorporate a circus environment. Like with Born Again Michael, I was ignorant to the conventions of this particular genre, so I approached it in a way that would skirt any established tropes. Here, I let the somewhat gimmicky concept of an all-dialog story become the center of the story, rather than the circus in which it is set.

Dialog, as exposition, became perhaps more of a challenge than learning about the circus to begin with would have been. It is important to me that my writing never comes across as pure gimmick. I try new things all the time (my novella, *As a Machine and Parts*, is illustrative and plays with text in unusual ways), but I always want to ensure that I'm not being strange for the sake of strange. I want to be strange for the sake of the story. The focus on dialog works with It Sparks because the story is centered around two people—a father and a son—talking to each other about generational differences as they watch what the father refers to as a "so called circus." I was able to dodge the expectations a bit, as a story about the circus practically demands visual details. But because I refrained from those types of details, and offered only verbal queues, the reader is forced to hang onto each word a bit tighter than she might otherwise.

This must be how genre writers feel; they have a set of rules and must stretch into new territory without breaking those rules. Perhaps more vampire stories are coming my way.

Car Dodging

Car Dodging leads with easily one of the most polarizing intros I've ever written. Though the concept of welcomed rape is admittedly shock-driven to an extent, it still serves the greater story. A lot of people find this opening sexist. Those people probably stopped reading after the opening and therefore have no business commenting.

This story is based on an actual game my friends and I played during our Junior High-ish years. Unlike the story, we had no point system, and the drivers were considerably more furious in real life, but nonetheless the "real" game carried all the absurdity of the "story" game. Our goal then, and during much of our pre-High School days were motivated by a desire to edge ever closer to that line that would finally force us to accept our mortality. Nobody ever got hurt car dodging, so as far as we were concerned death was just a parental scare tactic. We also spent plenty of time throwing Christmas lights from atop Osage City main street storefront roofs and lighting things on fire. Death never came.

An early version of this story won the Kay Alden Creative Writing Scholarship during my years at Emporia State University. By that time I had stopped going car dodging, which is good because, though the scholarship money was quite helpful during my minimum wage college years it definitely wouldn't have paid for the repair of a cracked skull.

Snake Girl at Scab

I remember being scared that my wife would read this story and somehow overlay our own lives with the lives of Eric and Lacy. I also remember having no reason at all to be scared about that. Snake Girl at Scab, if I remember correctly, was one of the first domestic fiction (re: Kitchen Sink drama) pieces I had ever written, so without the usual dismemberments and deformities it is easier to retroactively understand how a story like this might seem a bit too "normal" in context, too normal *not* to imply the author's own domestic life. It probably doesn't help that story's snake girl, though definitely not the female interest in the story, still was based on an actual person I saw wandering a weekend art show in Portland, Oregon.

This piece has meaning for me outside the story itself, too. This was my first (and only, as of today) piece of fiction published at 3:AM Magazine. Early, when I first began writing seriously, 3:AM was high up on a dream list of online fiction sites I hoped to break into.

Norman Rockwell Nostalgia

Like *Stranger Will*, Norman Rockwell Nostalgia has unexpected political roots. I wrote briefly, at The Nervous Breakdown, about *Stranger Will*'s origins in my own disenfranchisement with the early 2000's political climate, and how the Middle East occupation spawned in me what I would come to understand as a version of the philosophy of apatheism. Part of this philosophy is learning to realize that 'the good 'ol days' never existed. *Leave it to Beaver* was just as much an idealized romantic view of domestic life back in the late 50's and early 60's when it was created as it was during every subsequent decade that it aired in syndication. *Leave it to Beaver*, *The Andy Griffith Show*, *Lassie*, *I Love Lucy*, these shows were not documentaries. I was slowly becoming upset with the too-easily accepted false nostalgia among political leaders that seemed to indicate that these TV shows—and similar forms of cultural references such as the images depicted in Normal Rockwell paintings—were factual documents representative of a forgotten innocence in our country. Various versions of "we need to get back to our roots," and "look at how bad things have gotten," became talking points for government leaders obsessed with placing blame for "forgetting our roots" and "making things so bad" on political opponents.

My doctor has a series of Norman Rockwell prints hanging throughout the halls of her office. My blood pressure rises every time I enter. I blame those images for my doctor believing I have the heart of a 50 year-old.

Help an author

Please, click over to Amazon.com, Goodreads, Facebook, Google+, YouTube, Twitter, and any other of your online homes and spread the word of this book and of me, the author, Caleb J. Ross. Authors have no marketing budget. Therefore, we depend on readers like you to share the enthusiasm of books in order to keep our highballs full and our pints stout.

About the Author

Caleb J. Ross has a BA in English Literature and creative writing from Emporia State University. His fiction and nonfiction has appeared widely, both online and in print. He is the author of five books of fiction and is the creator of Burning Books, a YouTube channel featuring humorous book reviews, literary skits, writing advice, and rants.

Homepage   Calebjross.com
YouTube   Calebjross.com/youtube
Twitter   Calebjross.com/twitter
Facebook   Calebjross.com/facebook
Google+   Calebjross.com/Google

www.ingramcontent.com/pod-product-compliance
Lightning Source LLC
Chambersburg PA
CBHW030545130626
46552CB00006B/2435